# A BED FOR BEAR

WRITTEN AND ILLUSTRATED BY
## CLIVE McFARLAND

**HARPER**
*An Imprint of HarperCollinsPublishers*

A Bed for Bear

ISBN 978-0-06-223705-7

The artist used Caran d'Ache Neocolor II and Winsor & Newton watercolors
on 98 lb Canson Mi-teintes paper and merged them in Photoshop
to create the digital illustrations for this book.
Typography by Rachel Zegar
14  15  16  17  18    SCP    10  9  8  7  6  5  4  3  2  1

First Edition

For Finn, Hope, and Ophelia

# IT WAS NEARLY WINTER,

and Bernard was getting sleepy. It was almost time for the bears to begin hibernating.

There was just one problem. How could Bernard possibly be expected to sleep in the bear cave? It was too noisy, too big, and too crowded.

That kind of place was right for some bears . . .

. . . but not for Bernard.

So Bernard did what any bear without a bed would do. He set off to find a new place to sleep.

Bernard knew there had to be a bed that was just right for him.

Bernard walked into the forest.
There he met Frog.
"Hi, Frog. I'm looking for a new
bed. Can I try your lily pad?"

"Sure, Bernard. Hop on."

"Wet isn't very comfy."

"Sorry, Bernard. It's hard to hop on
a lily pad. This kind of bed is right for
frogs but not for big bears like you."

Bernard kept walking. Then he came across Bird.

"Hi, Bird. I hear you have a great bed. Can I try out your treetop?"

"Climb on up, Bernard."

"I'm sorry, but windy doesn't feel right."
"You get used to it, Bernard. . . ."
"I don't think so, Bird."

"I guess this kind of bed is right
for birds but not for bears."

Bernard saw Rabbit on his way
back to the burrow.
  "Hi, Rabbit. Your bed looks quite
nice. Can I try your burrow?"

"There's really not a lot of
room, Bernard."

"You're right. This is a tight fit."

"I tried to warn you. This kind of bed is
right for rabbits but not for bears."

Bernard kept walking. He stumbled
into Hedgehog soon after.
"Hi, Hedgehog. Where's your bed?"
"I sleep right here."
"What happens if it rains?"
"I get wet."

"Oh, well, that's probably fine
for hedgehogs," Bernard said,
yawning, "but not for a bear."

Bernard was getting sleepier and sleepier. Luckily, he came across what looked like a fine place to lie down.

"This bed looks comfy even if it is a bit lonely. . . ."

Bernard was not alone for long.

"Bernard? What are you doing in my bed? A badger sett is no place for bears."

"Why not?"

"Because it's *for badgers.*"

Bernard didn't know where else to look.
He was getting ready to give up when a
little voice asked,
"What kind of bed DO you want?"

"Well, that's simple. You see, I need a bed
that is not wet, not windy, extra roomy,
with just the right amount of company!"

"I think I know a place for you."

Up ahead, there was a rather interesting bed. It was dry and calm, with lots of space and plenty of company.

This kind of bed was okay for some bears . . .
but it was perfect for Bernard.

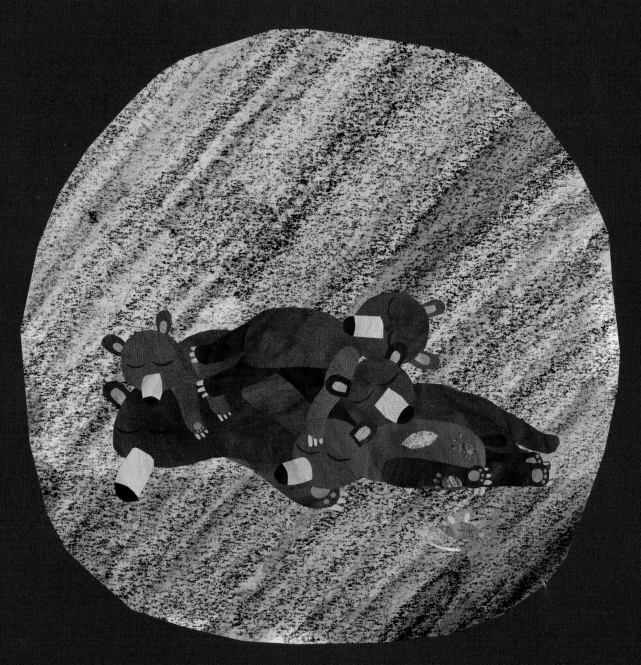

Bernard slept, all winter,
in a perfect bed for a bear.